strange shorts

strange shorts

Rowena Holloway

FRACTURED PRESS PTY LTD
ADELAIDE

contents

vii

Introduction   1

1. Butterflies   5

2. Weylin's Lament   9

3. Shattered   17

4. Grave Surprise   23

5. When Billy Went Beetroot   29

6. A Sensible Girl   37

7. Letter Home   47

8. Progress   51

9. It's a Commin', Dottie   57

10. The Weight of Years   65

                                                     67

Pieces of a Lie   69
First Chapter Extract

                                                     79

All That's Left Unsaid   81
First Chapter Extract

                                                     87

Ashes to Ashes   89
First Chapter Extract

Acknowledgements   97
About the Author   99
Praise for Rowena Holloway   101

For Bill, Yvonne and Buddy
Thanks for all the beach walks and talks
and for your faith in my writing journey

introduction

Strange Shorts. It seems the most fitting name for this collection. The stories are short—between three hundred and twelve hundred words—and they are all a little strange. When I wrote them I had no idea they were strange though it shouldn't have been a surprise to discover they were. I've always been drawn to the dark and quirky. I grew up surrounded by English folklore and devoured tales of ghosts and other-worldly happenings and often draw inspiration from these, particularly for short stories.

Once all these disparate stories were collated and I read them through as one, I realized many were about family and relationships—no surprises there—but they were also about love, sometimes freely given and uncomplicated, but most often complicated. The biggest surprise to me was the theme that seemed to run through all of them: the shifting perspective of truth.

The nature of truth runs through nearly everything I write, and is most certainly at the heart of my novels, though I have never consciously decided to write around that theme. Possibly it's my subconscious at work. Natalie Goldberg talks about the importance of not shying away from what comes up through fear of what you might discover. Great advice. It can, however, be a little harrowing when you see what emerges on the page.

The stories in Strange Shorts were written over several years. Some are just musings written as writing exercises while others have won or placed in literary competitions.

You'll notice that 2011 was a particularly successful year. That year I took a break from novel writing to concentrate on short stories. It was also my year of 'going for it'. It was the first time I attended the Romance Writers of Australia Conference and though I did feel like a cuckoo in the romance nest I got a lot out of the sessions, including the advice about submitting as much as possible in any given year. Buoyed by that advice and by an early draft of one of my novels reaching the top 1% in a huge international literary competition in 2010, I submitted more than fifty stories to various competitions in Australia and around the world.

It was a good strategy though exhausting and not always with the result I'd hoped for. Just like dating, you have to kiss a lot of frogs to find a prince!

I must confess to feeling a little nervous about sharing some of these stories—the untried ones and the ones that didn't get picked up for awards—but then I remind myself that self-belief is important. If I enjoy them then hopefully you will too.

Happy reading

Rowena Holloway

I

butterflies

Annie is dreaming of the lost little girl when the butterflies wake her. The breath of their fairy wings a call to play as they flit and dance at her window. Mother said when she wakes early, when the sun still has one eye shut, she must wait.

Wait till mother comes for you, Annie. Don't go off alone.

But Annie doesn't like to wait. Not today. Today she is a big girl. Ten years old. Old enough for the big knives and forks. Old enough to decide what to do with her day. And for breakfast today there will be pancakes—if she waits. Waiting is hard. Almost as hard as the sums Mother gives her. The numbers never stay still long enough for Annie to know them. *Come on, Annie,* they say, *let's go outside and play.* And they slip away off the page running across the table and out the door and Annie skips after them laughing.

Mother gets angry. And sometimes she gets sad, so sad that big dollops of water fall from her eyes. Once, Annie watched them roll down her cheeks and splash onto the table. That was the day Annie went to the river alone. She stayed until the sun shut both its eyes and then she couldn't find her way home because the white picket fence she'd followed wasn't white enough and she wasn't sure it was the same. After that Mother said she must wait. That she mustn't go outside without permission, that she must never-ever-ever go to the river alone because a long, long time ago a little girl was lost there and her mummy waited and waited, but she never came home.

Annie aches to find that lost little girl.

Wait until mother comes with you, Annie.

Annie thinks all this as she pulls on her dress and buckles her sandals. But the butterflies are calling softly. *Come with us Annie. Come dance with us.* And they are so pretty and delicate and free. And with the butterflies she won't be alone.

Mother hears the back door slam, hears the laughter of her sweet, damaged Annie. She knows it's a dream and pulls the covers higher. Just a little longer. Today is a big day. Lots of Annie's friends are coming and there is much to do, but a few more moments won't hurt. And she likes dreaming of Annie laughing.

Annie's laughing as she chases the butterflies down the path and out the front gate. They dance past Mrs Brown's store where mother buys the apples she likes, past the one-eyed dog sleeping on the post office steps, past the picket fence. The butterflies show her the dew on the leaves. It glistens, like the tears on Mother's cheeks. Mother. For a moment Annie stops dancing. She looks back along the dusty road to the little house with the rusting roof. A little way up the street Ned kicks up red dust as he pulls the milk cart. She likes Ned. Likes the silken feel of his mouth on her palm when she shares her apple, likes the clip, clop of his hooves when he reaches the sealed road that runs into town.

Wings of red and gold flit across her vision. Butterflies!

Annie turns. They are dancing up ahead, their wings so pretty in the brightening light. Annie runs and runs but she can't quite catch them. She knows where they're taking her. To the big tree with the tyre swing. To the river.

When she reaches the water's edge they dance out across the rippling surface, far out in the middle of the river, out where the water is bluer, where it moves faster.

Out where the lost little girl waits for Annie.

weylin's lament

The news came by way of a rare letter from Keith. A single line in a page filled with words about the lad's world so far from his roots: indexes, stock movements, and how the trebled price of commodities and increased demand for steel meant that an earthquake was lucky. Weylin understood the words, it was the sentiment he couldn't fathom.

He set his chisel aside and removed his foot from the pedal of the lathe. Sweet-scented sawdust carpeted the floorboards, and just beyond his workshop doors geraniums quivered in the breeze while in the valley below sunlight brightened the whitewashed walls. Last night the low moon had silvered the gleaming headstones and the ancient Elder standing twisted and proud in the cemetery.

An omen. He knew that now.

Sometimes it was easy to believe he was the last man left in these mountains. Just him and his fine creations, and the dark mass that hovered on the edge of his sight.

Would Keith come when it was done?

He worked the pedal until the piece of two-by-two spun to a blur. Working the timber brought him closer to happier times when Keith loved the woods behind his home and spent his days climbing trees or fishing from the stream. In those days the glen was filled with the boy's laughter. Weylin remembered his lad's easy gait, his generous heart, the way his little face glowed with eagerness to learn the ways of his ancestors. Many happy hours he'd spent teaching his son knowledge gathered through countless generations.

They were lost to him now, those days of delight.

If only they hadn't sent him away to school.

If only the boy had listened.

Weylin pumped the pedal and lifted his chisel. He sensed more than saw the smoke-like tentacles reaching for the timber, but knew if he turned his head she'd be gone. It was only ever a glimpse. A threat. A promise.

"Not yet," he said. "Not yet." It had to be done right.

Likely the lad still denied the truth of what happened that day in the woods. Likely he wasn't troubled by the horror that Weylin relived nightly, tortured by the drip-drip-drip on the black earth. That sound filled his dreams, sometimes his days too.

This was his last chance to set things right.

He'd known the day was close even before he visited that fancy doctor. As soon as he'd returned from the city he'd gone into the woods and found the place where it had happened. The scars hadn't healed. The doc had reeled off a list of twenty-dollar words but when Weylin saw those scars so deep in the trunk he knew the shadow on his lungs had nothing to do with smoking.

That day in the woods Keith had accused him of being a 'culchie'. It was a word Weylin hadn't understood until Keith had sneeringly explained.

"A culchie, is it?" Weylin cried. "Have you

forgotten you're a culchie? You're a country lad all the way through to your bones. Just like me and your dear Ma. Or aren't we good enough for you now? Two years with city folk and you're too good for your own people, are you?"

The boy stayed mute and kicked at the mulch beneath his large feet; at fifteen he was already a hulking lad. Weylin had feared he'd throw more than insults.

"Go find yourself a good strong branch,' he'd told Keith, 'something with a bit of flex. And remember what I taught you."

Keith had stomped off, scuffing up the earth, a sure sign he'd forgotten all he'd been taught. Weylin hadn't recognised the signs. Instead he'd found himself a sturdy branch and was halfway through his ritual when there came a howling through the trees. The following shrieks were enough to put his heart crossways. His lad appeared clutching a thin branch that was still so green and moist its ragged end bled upon the earth.

Weylin stared in horror as rotting leaves and twigs whirled around them. "Boy, what have you done?"

Keith threw down his makeshift fishing pole.

As soon as the branch hit the undergrowth leaves whirled up, faster and faster, until it seemed like the world was made of them. They whipped at the boy, smacking his face and clothes as he ran for the edge of the woods, yelling, his arms flailing as he tried to protect himself.

With a last pump of his foot Weylin blew the dust away and caressed the spinning leg until it calmed beneath his touch. The final piece was ready. He set to work marking and chiselling the voids so that the pieces fit together like a jigsaw. As he worked, the shadow trembled. She was growing, reaching out to him. A sense of unease niggled.

"It's got to be done. The boy needs reminding."

All these years the dark mass he'd glimpsed from the corner of his eye hadn't just hovered. A piece of it had taken root in his lung. All his efforts to make amends had been wasted. Yet he'd returned from the city determined to set things right, hoping it wasn't too late for Keith.

He fitted the last piece and stepped back. He'd made a fine job of the sacrificed Elder tree, but as he admired his work the looming mass swirled around the crib.

Perhaps he was going too far.

As though sensing his uncertainty, the dark apparition reached out and curled around his face, stoking his cheek as Mary once had in their most tender moments. Then it disappeared into the timbers of the crib.

If only Keith had asked permission that day in the woods.

"You've always got to ask, lad," he'd warned. "You never take even a twig without allowing the tree to give it to you of its own free will."

"How do I ask?"

"You tell the tree your need and then you wait."

"For what?"

"For silence. You'll know soon enough if the tree takes umbrage."

"What happens if I take it anyway?"

"Then the Tree Witch'll come for you. You 'specially don't want to take from the Elder tree or Hilde-Moer will cause you no end of trouble until you set things right."

Few believed in the Tree Witch now. They looked at the Elder tree and its tangle of branches and saw something ratty to be removed from gardens. Perhaps that was the cause of the world's ills—no one asked permission anymore.

That day in the woods he'd tried to make it right. He'd begged forgiveness for what Keith had done, asked her to heap vengeance on his own weary head.

It was Keith she wanted.

He packaged up the crib and its dark passenger. Young Frank from the village would be by to pick it up. It was all arranged. There was nothing more he could do but hang on to his faith that the man who had once been the joyful boy who'd gobbled up his teachings would remember the ancient lore and set things right, as he should have done all those years ago. Keith had a responsibility now to teach his own boy and continue the ways of his people.

I'm very sorry, the specialist had said. *Best get your affairs in order.*

Waylin took one last, loving look at his workshop, at the carpet of sawdust and the well-used lathe. Then he turned his back on all he'd held dear and shuffled toward the woods.

Not for him the slow disintegration in a box in the cold earth.

3

shattered

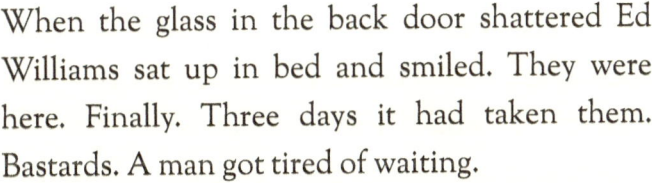

When the glass in the back door shattered Ed Williams sat up in bed and smiled. They were here. Finally. Three days it had taken them. Bastards. A man got tired of waiting.

Ed shifted to the side of the double bed and slid his bony legs from beneath the covers. The bright edge of a full moon shone through the tear in the blind and turned his pale skin grey. He should've guessed they'd come on a full moon. Not an ounce of sense among the lot. He'd known that by looking at them.

A hollow thud. They'd closed the kitchen door. Now they'd be creeping up the hallway, past his stacks of newspapers, probably pull out the phone jack just to be sure. Though why they'd bothered to close the kitchen door like that was beyond him. They knew it was warped. The thick-headed kid had struggled with it just the other day.

For a moment Ed doubted his certainty. What if it wasn't them?

Of course, it was. He'd seen how much they wanted the damn thing, though they'd told him it was worthless. If they hadn't lied to him, he might have given it to them and been glad to see the back of it.

In the heavy silence Ed heard laboured breathing. His. The heart that had seen him through a world war and years of struggle pounded so hard it was like a fist against his chest. He hadn't reckoned on being frightened. The cricket bat was near the door. It seemed a lifetime away. Should've kept it near his bed where he could grab it quick smart, but he'd always been a stubborn bugger. His Ailsa had been right about that. She'd been right, too, about that God-awful thing she'd lugged home from the market all those years ago. Could've blown him over with a kiss when he saw how much they wanted it.

With his feet planted on the rug Ed heaved himself upright and reached for the dressing gown hanging on the back of the dresser chair. The night was sultry, but he wasn't about to confront these no-hopers clad only in his cotton PJs. The kitchen door thudded again. Bloody hopeless. They probably reckoned on him sleeping without his hearing aids or cowering under his sheets. Ha! They didn't know Ed Williams. But that was the whole point—that they didn't know diddly about Ed Williams.

He shuffled across the threadbare carpet, feeling his way past the foot of the bed, ears open to any sound from the rear of the house.

The clatter of tin on stone. That'd be the fire surround he'd placed in front of the lounge room door. Any halfway decent thief would have been on the lookout. Not these idiots. No finesse in kids today. In his heyday he could've shown them a thing or two. Back then he could face down grown men with just a squint of his bright-blue eyes.

Ed reached the bedroom door and wrapped his stiff fingers around the handle of the cricket bat. The cloth wrapping was damp and missing in parts where the rats had gnawed it. It wasn't the best weapon he had. His old Luger was in an

Arnott's biscuit tin on the top shelf of his wardrobe, but after years of inactivity the bat was less likely to explode in his face.

A sliver of light fell across his bedroom carpet. They'd turned on a lamp to look for their spoils.

Now that they were here his faith almost deserted him. For three nights he'd left his bedroom door ajar, he and the cricket bat ready and waiting, yet now as he stood in the lee of the door, cricket bat raised, his entire body trembled.

They were whispering now, probably wondering what he'd done with it. He'd hidden his medals too. After the way that half-wit kid had ogled them it was a sure thing they'd get nabbed as well, and he hadn't slogged through mud, disease and dead mates to let some nose-wipe steal the only things that made up for it.

The hallway filled with the thuds of overturned furniture, the crash of things being smashed. Ed hadn't cared about any of it. Not for years. It was just crap on which his silly wife had frittered their savings, yet something like grief filled him with every crack of furniture, every smashed ornament. It was too much. He yanked open his bedroom door.

"Come on, you bastards. Show yourselves."

Ed Williams wouldn't go down without a fight, even if the bastards were his own kin.

4

grave surprise

With the whiskey bottle hugged to me chest, I quit me singin' and strained me ears. An owl hooted. A dog yelped. In the chilly breeze the leaves rustled.

Imaginin' things, Seamus? With a warmin' slug from me bottle I got set to pick up me singin'.

There it was again. A squealing.

Ah, tis the church door, to be sure. Know those squeakin' hinges anywhere. It'd be the Father. Though what he was doin' in church past midnight with nary a villager in sight was between him and his maker.

In me little hidey-hole I huddled into me patched coat and blessed the good ladies of *Tamlaght Mhor* for me woollen stockin's. The Father wouldn't care to find me here. *Graves are fer the dead, Seamus,* he'd said, but after bein' stung like that in front of the whole village I ain't keen to show me face to anyone. Such a lot of hollerin', there was, though any feller could tell I didn't mean to do it. It had nothin' at all to do with the whiskey.

Whatever the Father was carryin' was rattlin' like a drainpipe in a storm.

"Shush yer noise," a voice said. "Do yer want to give us away?"

"There's no one here but the dead, Fergus."

"Don't be an arse. Didn't yer hear the singin' before?"

"Singin'? In this weather! A voice from the grave, is it? The dead ain't gonna rise up now, are they, Fergus?"

"Don't be an arrr—"

A big feller landed smack-bang at me feet. Before I could tip me cap to him he started yellin' fit to split me ears. So I grabbed me shovel and whacked the feller flat in the face. That ceased his squawkin'. He grabbed at me but I whacked him again and he staggered back.

"Dermot! Dermot," the feller called. "Get me outta here!"

A pink face showed above us. "Yer should see yerself, Fergus. Haven't seen yer lookin' like that since Bridie thought she were up the duff."

"Dry yer arse. Get me outta here."

The pink-faced feller was laughin' so hard that when he reached down to help the big one a sack landed at me feet. I saw with me own eyes the reason for the clatterin'.

At last, the good Lord had sent me a chance at redemption.

I hooked me foot on a tree root, flung meself onto the grass and was behind a lichen-clad headstone before the gougers could say, 'stung'. Just then the Lord saw fit to pelt the earth with freezin' rain—and me with me whiskey left in me hidey-hole!

The big one threw up the janglin' loot and the other pulled him out of the hole.

"When rain falls on an open grave," chanted the pink-faced one, "'tis the Devil come to take a life."

"Quit yer superstitious shite, Dermot."

That got me an idea. I laid me shovel against

the headstone three times, each with a clang fit to bring down the saints from heaven.

"Sweet Mary, mother of God, save us," prayed the pink-faced one. "Three knocks and no one there tis death, sure as the rain in the grave."

Three times more I belted me shovel against the headstone. If their breeches had been on fire they couldn't have scattered faster. The sack hit the ground.

"A-live, alive o-oh. A-live, alive o-oh..." Nicely warmed from the drink, me voice bounced off the church walls.

Dogs set to barkin'. Lanterns flared. Voices filled the night.

The big feller raced for the fence. Then he was up and perched on the iron railings, but when he jumped, the baggy legs of his strides caught fast on the fence spike. He hung there, upside down, his arse as bare as the day he greeted the midwife.

The pink-faced one doubled-up, laughin'. I took me chance, swung me shovel at his pointy chin and sent a tooth flying.

"Ferguth! Ferguth," he screamed, "the devil'th come for me. Ferguth!"

As he tried to stand and run, I whacked his backside with me shovel. He grabbed the tangled weeds and tried to scramble through the mud. Me shovel knocked him flat.

The Father was first on the scene followed by the local peeler. Saving the big one from his predicament, the peeler asked, 'How d'you get all these bruises, lads? D'yer take to each other with the candlesticks?'

The Father stepped away, clutching his precious altar goods.

"T'was the grave digger," the big one mumbled. "Took after us with a shovel, he did."

The peeler laughed. "Tell us another one, Fergus O'Malley. There ain't been a grave digger here since before you was born. Not since Seamus got ossified and took a header into that poor babby's grave. Split his noggin clean open, he did."

I shook me head at that. Those peelers they all kiss the blarney.

———————

Commended Eastwood Hills FAW 2011

Published in the Seaside Writers Anthology 2011

when billy went beetroot

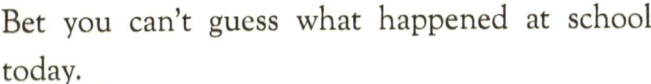

Bet you can't guess what happened at school today.

We had a new teacher.

Wow. Damien Schultz reckons she was smokin'.

Our regular teacher, The Gremlin—her name's not really Gremlin. It's Gremlich. But we all hate her 'cos she's mean and smells funny, so we call her The Gremlin—well, she was off at some meeting, so we got this new student teacher for the math's test. That's the test that's supposed to decide what class we go into in high school.

You should've seen all the boys staring at the new teacher. Billy Mumford, he got an eyeful down the new teacher's blouse and went so red we thought steam was gonna come out of his ears. But that was later—after he totally freaked.

The new teacher was just about to sit down when Billy leapt out of his chair so fast he nearly knocked over his desk. His maths book went flying and smacked Fat Mandy in the back of the head so hard it knocked the gobstopper out of her mouth and it landed smack on the front of the new teacher's shoe.

Damien Schultz thought that was hila-a-a-rious.

Anyway, Billy was standing there in the middle of the room with his school shirt all hanging out and his big shorts flapping around his knees and the teacher goes, "What's wrong with you?" and he goes all pink and says, "Er . . . Spider."

Well, the whole class cracked up—except for Shauna, who was hiding behind her emo fringe and texting—'cos Billy's nearly as big as a doorway *and* he's the school wrestling champ.

Billy goes to us, "Shut-u-u-p." And the teacher says she'll have none of that and for Billy to get his book and sit down. Then she goes to sit in her chair again and Billy yells, "No-o-o-o," and the new teacher looks at him, her eyes all big like one of those Bratz dolls, and Billy says, "The spider, it's on your chair," and the new teacher dances around and screams like she just saw Freddy Krueger.

Well, the whole class cracked up. Except for Shauna—who was texting—and that kid Mikey Bradshaw, the one who used to be friends with Billy Mumford, but now they're not talking 'cos Billy reckons Mikey's a douche bag now he wears a hoodie and his pants halfway down his bum.

The new teacher looked like she was gonna cry and she says for Billy to tell her his name and to get his book and sit down. So Billy goes to get his book, but Fat Mandy won't give it to him and Billy's going, "Give i-i-i-t," and Mandy just pokes out her tongue, which was bright blue from the iceblock she had a recess, and Billy called her a lizard face. So she stuck his book under her bum and sat on it. Billy goes, "Keep it lizard face. I'm not touching it now. Gross." And the new teacher tells Billy to sit down and by the way she still hasn't got his name. And Mikey goes, "It's Billy Munster, but we all call him Mummy's Boy."

Well, the whole class cracked up—except for Shauna who was texting—'cos we all call him Billy Munster behind his back and now that Mikey and him aren't friends anymore we all know the story of 'Mummy's Boy'.

See, when Billy went to Kindy—that's where him and Mikey made friends—his mum gave him a big kiss at the gate and started crying, and Billy was running across the yard where all the other kids were playing when his mum goes, "Be a good boy, Billy. Remember, you're Mummy's boy." So then everyone started calling him Mummy's Boy.

Billy hates it.

So when Mikey says it, Billy yells, "Shut up, Douche Bag. Shut u-u-u-p." And the new teacher she gets real angry and says she's gonna send Billy to the Head Mistress's office with a note about his behaviour. And she yanks open the desk drawer—the one where The Gremlin keeps her pens and pencils and all the things she's taken off us—and stuff goes *everywhere*.

Well, the whole class cracked up—except for Shauna who was texting—'cos someone had put the drawer in upside down and now there's toys and rubbers and pencils going everywhere.

The new teacher, she's real mad by now, and she's trying not to cry and her skirt is so tight she can't bend over properly so she's kind of crouching and trying to pick up everything. And Billy jumps up, knocking over his chair, and goes to help her—after he punched Fat Mandy in the arm and called her a lizard face again.

So Billy's got an armful of stuff and he goes to pick up a whiteboard marker that's rolled under the desk, but when he tries to pick it up it jumps out of his fingers, like it's on a piece of string or something. Mikey calls him a Doofus and Fat Mandy joins in. So the two of them are going, "Doofus, Doofus," and Billy's trying to pick up the pen and it keeps leaping out of his fingers like a slimy frog and the whole class is cracking up.

So the new teacher goes over to Billy and tells him thanks and he can sit down.

And that's when it happened.

She had on this white shirt and one of the buttons had come undone and when she leant over and held out the drawer for Billy to drop the stuff into, Billy copped an eyeful.

Damien Shultz goes, "On ya, Billy," and starts

clapping and Mikey joins in and even Shauna looks up from her texting. The new teacher looks all confused and then she notices her button is undone and what the class can see, so she grabs her shirt and orders Billy back to his chair, like it was his fault her shirt had come undone.

By now the whole class is watching and Damien and Mikey are clapping and whistling and some of the kids are laughing and Shauna's looking at Billy like he's the grossest thing she's ever seen. And Billy just stays there, on his knees, half crouched over, his face going pink.

The new teacher is practically crying now and she yells at Billy to go sit down and for the class to be quiet. But Billy doesn't move and his face is getting redder and redder. Which is when Terri and Jenni—those girls who always ring each other before school to make sure they dress the same—they start saying, "Billy better not have water on the brain 'cos otherwise he'll start whistling like a kettle."

Some of us heard that and we laughed and the teacher must have thought we were laughing at her 'cos she went up to Billy—who was nearly as tall as she was even though he was all crouched over—and she kind of gave him a shove.

Well, Billy didn't fall, cos he's used to stuff like that from wrestling, but he had to straighten up to steady himself and that's when we saw it.

At first everyone was dead quiet. Then we all cracked up.

That's when Billy went beetroot.

See, it looked like someone had pitched a tent in Billy's shorts.

Well, that was the end of the new teacher. We never did get to do our maths test. Not that anyone cared. Didn't see much of Billy after that either, though I did see him and Shauna behind the bike sheds, so I guess they're going out again.

They reckon when they find out who pulled all those pranks on the new teacher they're gonna suspend them and maybe make them repeat grade seven. I told them I'm pretty sure those pranks were meant for The Gremlin, 'cos no one knew we were getting the new teacher that day. But no one ever listens to me. If they did I could tell them who did it.

Oh it wasn't me. I'm not that clever. That's why I get to school early, so I can study. And that's when I saw who snuck into home room.

If they think about it they'll work it out. 'Cos who else would have made a dick of himself to stop a teacher sitting on a drawing pin except the person who put it there?

First Prize *Wyong Writers Not to Be Taken Seriously competition.*

Selected for inclusion in Award Winning Australian Writing 2011 published by Melbourne Books, Edited by Adolfo Arunjuez

6

a sensible girl

I'm a dreamer. Everybody says so. Mum's always telling me to get my head out of the clouds, and just the other day I overheard my employer, Mrs Allington, tell one of her boarders, "Saunders is a rather nice girl, but she's always dreaming."

Even my sweetheart, George, agrees. "Lottie, girl," he says, "it's all right for you to have your pretty head in the clouds so long as you keep your feet planted on the ground." He says he can't run the best garage in all of Adelaide with a wife who can't keep her mind on facts and figures. Owning a garage is George's dream. I tell him his dream is so real it's infected me. He just laughs. At least, he used to laugh, before he went off to war.

I bite into my apple. Cook said I should take a leg of chicken for my lunch by the Torrens, but that would only remind me of George and the picnic we had here the last time I saw him. So handsome in his uniform, he was. He told me I was to keep him tight in my heart so that I wouldn't forget him. I said I never could and kissed him, right there in the park where anyone could see. Later, on the crowded dock as the ship blew a warning, I kissed him again.

A baby's crying pulls me from my daydream. The young mother places the squalling baby in her perambulator and nods at me with a soft smile. Her name is Julia. She lives on the Lochend Estate and we've talked once or twice. Her man and George were among the first to enlist.

To take my mind off George, I watch the motorcars moving along Darley Road. Today, the first day of April sunshine, there are many people picnicking by the river and several cars parading by. George says them that can afford motors go past our special spot by the river to show off what hard work can do for a man. Mr. Viners, the butcher, calls George a dirty capitalist and says that it's the role of the working class to maintain the fabric of society. Mum says there wouldn't be no society without a woman to keep hearth and home, but I'd never repeat that to Mr. Viners.

John, who works at the garage which me and George are saving up to buy, he's been teaching me a little about engines. So far I've only really learned to crank-start a car. John says he'd bet sixpence to a penny that most motor problems start with a stall on account of the young ones don't know how to treat the machines. That's why he's teaching me to drive. My George will be so proud of his dreamy girl when he returns this Christmas. By then our boys would have brought an end to the Great War. All the papers say so. They said the same last year, but I'm sure this time they are right.

That day at the dock my handkerchief fluttered farewell as I smiled through the farewell cheers. My tears didn't fall until the ship was a dot on the horizon. If Mum had seen me bawling in public she would have scolded the skin off me, but nobody minded. All us girls were crying into our handkerchiefs: boarding house maids like me; smart girls in tiered skirts that showed their white-stockinged ankles; even old women in stiff black gowns with crow wings on their hats.

At my little spot by the river rainbow lorikeets chirp and swoop, landing on the branches then taking flight in a burst of chatter. I usually enjoy their games. Lately they are too much like Mrs Allington, who jumps at every pull of the doorbell. A peek through the curtains and any sign of a postal uniform is enough for her to collapse into a chair. "You go, Saunders," she says. "I can't bear it."

For over two months now there has been no word of Mr. Allington. He's over in Egypt like my George. I wrote George about him, but he wrote a short note back that infantry don't know much about them in the Light Horse.

Our resident boarder, Mrs Robinson, who is very active in the war effort, has told us that bad news will come by telegram, but Mrs Allington heard of a woman who got the CO's letter first and now she fears any kind of letter. Mrs Robinson says she should be more worried about the short rations, the mud and rats in the trenches, and the sickness that plagues those at the Front. She says it won't be long now before all those in Egypt are sent there. The doctor has told her she is not to speak of such things as it plays on Mrs Allington's mind so. Doctor says I must make sure my employer rests and to carry smelling salts with me at all times. Even now I have some in my pocket.

Before my George left and Mrs Allington got so weak, I would sit here in the park dreaming of a different life, of wearing white dresses with comfortable waists and lace hanging in points near my ankles. Once, on this very park bench, when there was no-one to see me, I lifted my skirts just a little. When the breeze caught my ankles, I blushed. It was as if I'd stepped out without my chemise.

I don't dream of fancy dresses anymore. I dream of George. I try to imagine what it's like for him.

A flash of red on the Darley Road—a beautiful motorcar with a long bonnet and open carriage roars past the others. Its engine sounds like one of those big cats George and me saw at the circus when we first stepped out. If only he was here to watch. He would tell me all about the motor then laugh at my interest and call me a tomboy, but he'd be ever so pleased. I know he would. Just as I know he'd be pleased if I could somehow join him.

Last month, I dared to ask Mrs Robinson if

there wasn't some way a girl like me could help with the war effort, that I'd heard tell of a woman driving an ambulance in Belgium. She turned to stare at me as I helped place the fox around her neck, for it was a fearful chilly day for March.

"Where do you get your ideas, girl?" She fixed me with a frosty eye. "The Government in its wisdom would never allow it. Quite right, too."

I kept my eyes low, for Mrs Robinson could stare a girl out of her wits.

"Knitting, girl!" she said. "Mittens, mufflers, socks. That's what they need." She turned away, tutting about the cheek of young girls today.

Julia's baby is crying louder now. "Time for his tea," she tells me, struggling to push the high wheels of the pram through the thick grass.

Every day I think of what Mrs Robinson had said about conditions at the Front. What must it be like for George, who only ever dreamed of keeping motorcars purring like kittens? When I told my Mum I wanted to help with the war effort she said I must leave that to my betters. I burst out that I could do what I liked if only I'd been a boy. She turned as pale as the turnip she was peeling.

"Well, I never," she said, two cherry spots on her thin cheeks. "To think I'd see the day when one of my own family thought they knew better than God as made them."

Since then I spend an extra hour every Sunday praying for my immortal soul. I'm dreadful sorry for what I said, but every day I see young women walking arm in arm wearing the short cloak and long white aprons of the nursing corps and I know our boys need more than mittens.

A horn blasts. A woman screams. The red motorcar has done the circuit and is now bearing down on Julia and her child. I'm on my feet and haring towards them, aware of the baby wrapped tight in his pram and the horror on the driver's face. Julia screams again. The car swerves. It clips the edge of the pram, tossing it aside. A tangle of blanket and wailing baby tumbles across the grass. Julia staggers and collapses. The motorcar jumps the curb, its big wheels biting into the earth before it lurches to a halt.

The squalling baby is red-faced but unharmed. I bundle him up and crawl toward Julia, hampered by the wriggling child and my heavy skirts. Shoes and boots crowd me. Voices rise and drown each other out. I order everyone to get back, half aware that Mum would be shocked to hear me speak so to my betters.

Julia is pale and silent as I check for injuries. She seems unharmed. I remember the salts in my pocket and wave them under her nose until she squirms.

Her eyes fly open. "My baby. My baby!"

I tell her that I have him. That everything is fine. A policeman is called. Julia and her baby are helped home while the young woman driving the car is let off with a warning. Soon there is nothing left to show for the event but the grass stains on my petticoats and the muddy tyre ruts.

The driver lays a delicate hand on my shoulder. "I say, you're a sensible girl to have in a crisis. I don't suppose you've considered nursing?"

"No, Miss. I mean . . ." I smooth my skirts and dare to raise my eyes to her. "I want to drive an ambulance."

"You can drive?"

"Yes, Miss. That is, I'm learning."

She fits the crank handle to the car and turns it three times. The car splutters but doesn't start. I show her what John has taught me. Soon the car is purring and she is perched on the driver seat, her silk scarf settled around her dark waves. Finally, she gazes down at me, taking in my grass-stained skirt. I stare at the rutted earth, waiting for the same reprimand I had from Mrs Robinson.

"Don't stand there daydreaming," she says. "Hop in. The Red Cross needs girls like you. I can't promise you an ambulance, but I can get you close enough."

———

Shortlisted *for Stringybark Australian History Award* 2011.

Published *in Yellow Pearl—Eighteen Short Stories Anthology 2012*

7

letter home

Dearest Robert,

It was wonderful to finally receive your letter. Do you know I got it just the other day? I know you must have written it soon after I left for my little holiday, so that means it took two months to reach me! Australia Post really has gone to the dogs, just as Great Aunt Maud always said. Honestly, you could have brought it quicker yourself. Oh, don't worry. I'm not having a go. I understand that you are so busy working that you can't come. Still, it would be lovely to spend some quality time together.

Everyone here is charming. I'm really

unwinding after all the stress of Christmas. You're right. Thirty people is too many and I should have let Janet do it. Still, we had a lovely time all things considered, didn't we?

Perhaps next time we won't invite the grandchildren. I know Christmas is all about children, but really, I had no idea they would go climbing through the cupboards. Thank goodness I spring cleaned! But how clever of them to find that funny looking vase in the back of your sock drawer. Oh, and those herbs they found rolled in a pair of your argyles were just the ticket for Jane's roast pork—finished it off a treat and didn't it look nice? It put everyone in such a good mood. They laughed and laughed. Of course little David looked a bit green, but he's always been a sensitive child, hasn't he?

It is good to know that Uncle Graham is feeling much better. He did eat rather a lot of turkey. Licked the bones clean. At one point I thought he was going to suck all the skin off his own fingers. Who would have thought such a mild-mannered man had so colourful a vocabulary? And the yelling! I suppose I should've have realised to thaw the turkey in the fridge, but it was a warm day and I knew it'd be much faster if

I just set it on the window sill. Poor man. Still, they tell me here that stomach pumps are much nicer than they used to be.

Fancy us taking two trips to Emergency in the same day? I do hope that Jerry's leg is on the mend. I know we've had our differences, but I thought with me doing Christmas and giving his Janet a break he'd finally warm up to me. I suppose I shouldn't have waxed the floor quite so thoroughly, but it did need it. And it looked so lovely with the table set and the floor gleaming. Perhaps I should have warned him, but I honestly didn't think he'd get around in his socks. Not on Christmas Day.

How is Stella? I have to admit that I was surprised to find her on our bed with your arms around her, but as you said, she was sick. I didn't think vegetarians ate turkey, but she did look rather flushed and dishevelled. You are always so kind to look after her. And yes, I suppose that with you so busy with work and Stella so eager to help out, it does make sense for her to stay at our house.

That nice lawyer fellow came to see me yesterday. He said I was looking very well. I agree that I'm very lucky to be here with all the lovely gardens rather than that dreadful grey cell where the police took me on Boxing Day. But the rooms here are terribly small. I've met some lovely people—though some are very strange—and Maggie (she's a doctor, you know) organises get-togethers every day so that we can talk about why we're here. It's all rather philosophical, I suppose. When I tell her my little holiday is almost over and I'm eager to get back home to you, she just nods and smiles.

Well, I have to go now, dearest. Lovely Miss Jones is here to take me to some kind of therapy. I don't know what that's all about, but I'm sure it'll be fun. Apparently they're worried about me biting my tongue during this therapy. I suppose I do talk a little too much. Before I go I do have one quick question: the lawyer said something about an annulment. What does he mean, dear? And what does he mean about you and Stella going to Barbados?

Write soon, dearest Robert. I know you'll explain everything so neatly. You always do.

All my love,
Susan.

8

progress

Don Bleacher mopped his brow with an oversized handkerchief, loosened his tie and released the top button of his business shirt. It was too damn hot to be walking in this wasteland at the peak of the summer heat. He should have stayed in the Beamer with the air-conditioning ruffling what was left of his hair, and his aching back supported by the ergonomic lumbar support and the butter-soft leather.

He would have if not for that interfering girl.

Usually, the opulence of his prized possession soothed him. His BMW was his reward for all the years of hard graft, all the palms he'd greased, all the pride he'd choked back in the name of progress. Eileen was part of that reward. She soothed his wounded soul and massaged his ego, as well as more pleasurable parts, but what he loved about Eileen—and he did love her—was her big laugh, the way she lived for gossip but never judged, and never shied away from an argument.

Although yesterday he could've done without that quality.

In his stagnant world of climate-controlled offices and check-box paperwork, Eileen was an ocean breeze. Perhaps that's why he'd come down to the river, to seek a little of the real thing. Because one thing was sure, the only breeze Eileen had shown him was the one when she yanked open her front door for him to leave.

Everything would have been fine if that damn girl hadn't shown up.

It had hurt him when Eileen challenged his feelings for her. Sure, some of his passion sprang from the illicitness of what they did, that's why it was called an 'affair', for Christ sakes. Yet what he and Eileen had was something more. He knew it. He was pretty sure she knew it. So it had been a blow to discover one accusation from that nosey girl had Eileen tossing down her needlework and showing him the door. He could still see the smug smile on the girl's face and the way Eileen's silk thread had spilled across the floor like bright red blood.

That girl was nothing but trouble. Her protests had held up his development of prime seaside land costing him a fortune in lost revenue and putting his schedule out by months. She'd scared off his major backer and now the council were back-peddling on their handshake agreement with his plans for the Prospect River Inlet when they'd been all over him a month before. That bloody girl and her protest group had scared the lot of them back into their holes. Weasels. And now the little bitch had set Eileen against him. As if he, Donald Douglas Bleacher, worth several million—on paper, at least—would waste his time threatening that group and its self-proclaimed leader. If he'd been that kind of thug he would have torched that heap of shit she called a car. The way he felt today, he might even have made sure to do it when she was inside.

All this thinking literally made him hot under the collar. The river chop suggested wind, but precious little touched his broiled skin. It was tempting to strip off and go for a swim though thanks to his development of Prospect Cove on the adjoining acres he'd give several people an eyeful. And that was a view they didn't deserve. After all, they paid top dollar to be in this prime precinct right on the river. To think, all that industry, all those people in newly created jobs—well, most of them were new—were here because he'd had the foresight and the balls to pull this town out of the dark ages. Maybe he should run for Mayor. Clean out that bunch of weasels who wasted everyone's time and council rates.

Don moved down onto the embankment in search of cooler air. With any luck he might see a dolphin. Maybe a mother and calf. There were rumours one of the local dolphins liked to dance on its tail. If anyone knew about his love for dolphins he'd deny it, but the truth was nothing made him prouder than knowing he had a significant hand in removing the industry that had fouled the river for more than a century. Water views and high-rise living were the way forward.

A sudden breeze whipped at the scrubland. About time. Yet this breeze carried something putrid.

Oh great. This was all he needed. Another prick trying his hand at illegal dog fighting over by the abandoned quarantine station. Some bugger had tried it a few years back, finding the isolation and flat scrub so close to the water the ideal place to run his game with a ready-made disposal for the dead dogs and plenty of warning if the cops came looking. At night, in that desolate place, you could see headlights for miles. The place stank like this then. Some weekends they'd find as many as three dogs—mostly staffys—tangled in the mangroves, their throats gone, their skin and ears mangled. Poor little buggers.

Nothing short of a vodka and tonic would sort him out today.

Don turned to climb the embankment and get back to work. He'd have to run the numbers, but with a bit of reclamation this ground would be perfect for expanding the Prospect Cove precinct.

He'd gone further down the embankment than he imagined. As he tried to climb, the bank sucked at his shoes like quicksand. Crap. Now he'd track all that muck into his car. He pushed himself forward, clutching at random vegetation to get some leverage, and had almost got back to *terra firma* when his foot snagged. He lost his grip and slipped through the muck on his belly. His legs hit the water with a splash and his foot jammed against a submerged log. Don rolled over and sat up. Mud covered him from knees to chin. And his foot—Holyfuckingjesuschrist!

It wasn't a log. It was a girl. *The girl.* straw-coloured dreadlocks snaked from her head like the mythical medusa. Sightless eyes no longer glared and her mouth—the mouth that had shouted such obscenities, the mouth that had planted doubt in Eileen—that mouth was sown shut with bright red thread.

9

it's a commin', dottie

Aled shoved his gnarled hands at his lower back and groaned. His back ached like it had in the war, when he'd carried a palliace and pack. A good night's sleep was what he needed; he'd been up all night listening.

"D'yer hear that, Dottie?" He'd sat straight up in bed, his heart doing a jig as the howl wrapped around their little cottage. "It's looking for someone to mark."

Dottie put her wide back to him. "Shush yer noise."

Aled heard it again and grabbed his wife's shoulder. "Gettin' closer, Dottie. It's a commin'."

"It's only the wind, yer scrut."

She jerked her shoulder free and tugged the bed clothes over her head. As if to make her point, she set to snoring fit to shake the bed to pieces. If she'd known he'd spent an all-night vigil at the window she'd have called him worse that a 'scrut'.

Aled sighed. For all her country slang, she wasn't Welsh born and bred. Not like him. She didn't understand the land and its ways. It had never soaked into her bones.

A draft waltzed a galaxy of sawdust across the workshop floor. It was gentle now, that wind. No more howl in its journey this morning. The harbinger never came in daylight. It rode the shoulders of the wind at night and liked a full moon best of all. Last night's had been a perigee moon. It had pushed its bright fingers beneath his shutters, lighting his way as he shuffled in his worn slippers, yet when he'd pushed open his shutters he hadn't been ready for the power of the luminous sphere so close he felt its touch.

"It's a commin', Dottie," he'd told her as she snored.

Aled smoothed his palm across the silky

timber of his latest creation. His hands were as dark and rough as the bark he stripped from the wood, too rough for Dottie, but the timber hummed beneath his caress. As gently as a lover's first kiss, he blew upon the curves and crevices he'd made with his chisel and savoured the sweet scent of the freshly made dust. Sawdust was his life force. He loved the carpet of it beneath his feet as he worked and the golden curls that clung to his boots when he planed.

"What do you think this is? A saw mill?" she once said to him, her hands fisted on her overblown hips. "Sweep up that mess. It's blowing in the house."

He'd said nothing, just quietly made a pair of doors for his workshop that fitted snug.

Those doors stood open wide today.

A hawk caught his eye. It hovered above the valley, eyes locked on some prey that might be oblivious to its fate, although the creatures of the valley heeded to nature's warnings as well as he did.

He stared across his hard-won patch of heaven at the town below, at the sharp angles of the buildings touched by early light. When the sun moved higher those walls would be as dull and impenetrable as the face Dottie showed him every morning across the kitchen table. From the thatched rooves below smoke twirled from the chimneys. Aled wondered how many of them down there had lain wide awake in the night listening to it howl, praying it would keep its distance. He bet the number would be more than would admit to it in the light of day, yet none of them would've kept vigil by their window as he had. They'd be too afraid it would show them his fiery eyes and lay its giant paw upon their heart.

"It's a commin', Dottie," he'd said as he stood at the window.

The Heleniums he'd planted for a bit of colour in the stony earth stood swayed with the breeze. *Weeds*, she called them, *ratty blossoms that make a mess no good woman should have to worry about.* She'd gradually pulled up every plant and flower around the house, but he'd put a stop to that when she started after his little plot. It was the first time in nearly half a century that he'd stood up to her. She'd huffed and slapped her gums a bit then marched into the house.

He lifted his chisel. The edge glinted, lethal and seductive. He set his foot to the pedal and pumped until the lathe began to turn. Then he gently touched the timber with the chisel.

Soon it would be time to harness Bess to the wagon. They didn't go into the village often, him and Bess. His craftsmanship made him something of a legend, but the villagers were quite content for eccentric old Aled and his ideas to stay up in the mountains. They loved his handcrafted furniture and made plenty of money selling it to the slick wheeler-dealers and tourists who came to see their quaint village, but they didn't understand his obsession with creating something from a slab of old tree. When he explained about freeing the angel from the marble, they looked at him with suspicion.

"But you ain't working with marble, Aled."

They didn't understand the peace he found as the machine hummed under his pedal power and the golden shavings curled at his feet. They couldn't fathom why an old boyo like him didn't buy the timber already stripped of its bark and sawn into nice neat strips. They couldn't feel the love he felt when he undressed the timber.

Sometimes he thought Dottie understood. Maybe that was why she'd been so determined to clear out his workshop. He'd come home and found her giving away his off-cuts and haggling with dealers over his half-finished pieces.

"Bloody rubbish," she said with a defiant lift of her chin. "It's cluttering up the place."

He'd stood up to her then too. In front of half the village. He'd picked his battles and won them both. Not so bad in a war that had been lost long before.

With a final pump of his foot Aled withdrew the chisel and blew the dust away. He caressed the spinning leg until it calmed beneath his touch. It was time to harness Bess. The burden would be heavier than usual, but they'd go slow and careful. That horse knew her way down that mountain even better than him.

The villagers would be surprised to see him, unless they were too busy looking sideways at each other. They might polish up the village, eradicate its bygone charms and slough off the old ways, but it was all for show. Just like his, their bones were soaked with the ancient lore. All those born-and-bred would be wondering who'd been marked by the devil's hound, who'd be taken within the year.

Aled understood that most times it didn't take a year. Sometimes it only took a moonlit night.

"It's a commin', Dottie," he'd warned. And he'd been right.

_____

Commended *FAWQ Lovers of Good Writing* 2011

Highly Commended *by Scribes Short Story Competition* 2011

IO

the weight of years

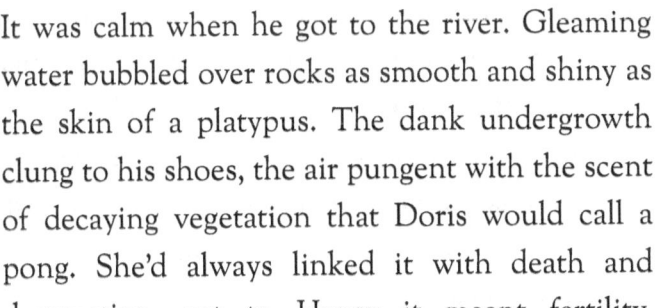

It was calm when he got to the river. Gleaming water bubbled over rocks as smooth and shiny as the skin of a platypus. The dank undergrowth clung to his shoes, the air pungent with the scent of decaying vegetation that Doris would call a pong. She'd always linked it with death and destruction, yet to Henry it meant fertility, growth, the end of one life nurturing another.

It turned out Doris didn't know anything about nurturing. She didn't understand it's importance.

'Things live and die,' she always said. 'Nothing we can do about it.'

And so the grapes withered on the vine, the garden beds became so desiccated that the little water God saw fit to send their way ran in rivulets across the parched earth.

But Henry knew. Knew a tree grew strong in fertile soil, that kids grew tall with good food and plenty of love. Dynasties lay in nurturing. It had little to do with the worship of the divine one day a week, the prayers for rain lost beneath the gossip on the steps of the old church.

Henry took off his shoes and folded his Sunday best over the bough of a gnarled tree older than the collective age of all those who had ever swung from its branches in summer. He let his tired feet sink into the bank's rich soil, let the slimy leaves and mud squelch between his toes.

This was the place. A place for a man to rest his weary bones and shed the weight of years he'd carried far too long.

One dark secret. Two troubled souls.

The lie that brings them together
could tear them apart.

pieces
of a lie

ROWENA HOLLOWAY

pieces of a lie

First Chapter Extract

'CAN'T YOU READ? Sign says private.'

The man's face flushed as he spoke, as though his arteries were so blocked the effort of speaking was too much. She'd seen the faded sign tacked to the door and ignored it. Just like she tried to ignore the whippet-thin teen sitting at the table, inching his wet tongue along pale, flaking lips. Sunlight through the blinds left shadowed bars across his face. Mina hugged the cardboard box she carried closer to her body and wished she'd worn her usual business shirt and trousers, not a thin summer dress that showed more skin than it covered.

'I want to buy these.' She rattled her box at the man whose silvered head nearly brushed the sloping ceiling. 'You don't even have to smile.'

'I ain't open for business, so clear off.' He shoved his arms up into his pits and glared.

'Go on, Kegs. Might make some cash for a change.'

'Shut it, Dunny, before I do it for yous.'

The kid lost his stupid grin and dropped his gaze to the jumbled assortment of brass and silver objects on the table. Tossed among the dull gleam was an old fob watch.

One, two, three, here we go. It's time—

She gasped at the sharp slap of memory and plucked up the watch. Some of the silvering had worn away. As her fingers curled around its edges, the brass felt warm and more familiar than it should.

'That ain't yours.' Thick fingers grabbed her wrist. 'Give it here. The watch ain't for sale.'

Mina twisted her arm free. 'I just wanted a look.'

The kid's gaze ran over her, his tongue busy as if he could taste her. In other circumstances she would have told him to take a picture, but this creep would probably take it as an invitation. The big one—Kegs—made another snatch at the watch, but she held it fast and moved out of reach. In a room this small, a man his size wouldn't get from behind the table without some effort, and his sidekick was too busy trying to peer through her dress to act.

She ran her fingers over the ridges on the watch cover, every bump as cold and smooth as she remembered, then she tilted the watch toward the window. The patterning came to life: a running dog, the bower of stars, the curving river at his feet. It couldn't be. Not here. Not now. She thumbed the clasp and the cover sprang open. The inscription was there. Just one word. *Forever*.

The floor seemed to slide from under her. She groped for a chair, clutching the watch, focusing on its solid feel, the reality of it, as her head filled with white noise.

'Does the picture mean something?' she'd asked her dad.

'The stream represents life,' he said. 'And the dog represents protection. My dad told me a story to go with it. It's the one I've told you, about the boy and his superhero dog.'

She'd wanted him to tell her again, but he wouldn't.

'We have guests, and lots to do.' He'd held out his hand for the watch and laughed when she'd tried to keep it. 'It'll be yours one day, Mina Mouse. Until then, it stays with me.'

And yet, here it was. In the back room of a country junk store, tossed aside like it meant nothing.

'Hey!'

A sweaty red face thrust close to hers. Stale odours of hair oil and unwashed skin wafted from his body. She was seated at the table. The chair hard beneath her buttocks. The lizard-tongued creep had hold of her hand, stroking it like she was his pet. She pulled herself free. In her other hand she still clasped the watch, slippery with perspiration.

'You think I got nothing better to do,' Kegs said, 'than stand here while you run your fingers over things that ain't yours?'

To think her heart had once trilled with excitement at the Sunday tea laid out, her mother smiling, the unbearable anticipation as they waited for him to spin a tale of bunyips or wombats or little girls who could slay dragons.

One, two, three, here we go, it's about time for the Everton show.

It was a show all right. Only her mother had clung to the fairytale, determinedly blind to the truth.

'Sometimes I think I love you and your mother too much,' he'd said that day.

'How can you love someone too much?' she asked. 'How do you know if you do?'

'When you'll do anything for them. Even when it's wrong.'

How prophetic that last statement had been. She didn't believe he'd done any of it out of love for her or her mother.

Kegs shoved his calloused palm at her. 'Hand it over, cupcake.'

Cupcake? That was a new one. She'd been called a few choice names before—buying up other people's keepsakes and selling them to the highest bidder wasn't always popular—but never cupcake.

'Leave off, Kegs. Can't you see she's sick?' The kid flicked his tongue. 'You're sick, hey, babe? You need to lie down.'

Lie down? Here? As if!

Kegs blocked her path to the door, his huge fists balled. He looked like he'd happily throw her out, but the other one...

Perspiration peppered her brow and dampened the back of her dress. Her pulse thudded. Why hadn't she told Forbes where she was headed? He'd nagged her often enough. She'd left her phone in her car and her keys were in her handbag, which was—where?

She spotted it on the floor beside the kid, resting neatly on its base, whereas her cardboard box had strewn its treasures across the scuffed floorboards. Kegs wasn't that much bigger than that slimy developer who was always at her to sell her house, and she'd faced him down more than once, enough to know creeps like these grew fat on fear.

'I'll give you fifty bucks for those.' She pointed at the scattered tea caddy spoons she'd unearthed from a pile of discoloured trinkets in a cabinet out front. They were worth one-hundred-a-piece to a collector, but to her they promised entry into a new life.

'Pick 'em up and I'll think about it.'

As soon as Kegs shifted, she shot from the chair and gathered up the spoons. She still gripped the watch. It had almost become part of her.

'Fifty bucks,' she said.

'Cash only, then piss off.'

'Aren't you even going to haggle? Must be hard doing business in a remote place like this.'

'What's it to you?'

She should have kept her surprise to herself. Guys like this always haggled. For most of them it was the only thrill they got, the reason they were in business.

'I want the watch too.'

'You deaf or something?'

'Look. It's rubbish.' She held the watch up to the light but stayed out of reach. 'Not worth a cent to a collector.'

'What's it to you, then?'

She shrugged. 'Feeling sentimental. My dad had one like it.'

'Go on, Kegs.' The kid winked at her as if they were co-conspirators, but his gaze dropped to her bare legs and once more his tongue got busy.

'Piss off.' Kegs grabbed her wrist, pried the watch from her fingers and tossed it on the table. It landed with a thunk. At some point they'd covered their horde with a limp tea towel. She pretended not to notice.

'Give me my bag.' She held out her hand.

'Give it to her, Dunny.'

The kid picked it up by the straps and dangled it just out of reach. It took everything she had not to grab it and run. She didn't need the watch to remind her of her father's lies—that legacy was there every time she walked down her street—but she did need those spoons.

From her purse she pulled out all the notes she had left and tossed them at Kegs. He caught some and began counting, sorting them into their five and ten dollar denominations. Dunny scrounged on the floor for the rest.

She risked a look at the table. From beneath the tea towel poked a striped ribbon, the kind usually attached to a medal. There was something familiar about it, something that made her skin crawl. She couldn't think why. She didn't know anything about medals.

'Ain't enough,' Kegs snapped.

'Of course it is.'

She'd had a busy day, but she could cover fifty in cash. Her credit card was maxed out. Besides, there was no way she'd hand over her card to these two. The less they knew about her the better.

She squared her shoulders. 'Take it or leave it.'

'I'll take it, you leave it.'

Kegs pocketed her cash then seized the spoons.

'Hey, I paid for those.'

'You didn't see no money change hands, did you, Dunny?'

'Nah, mate. And I reckon she owes us something for our trouble.'

Dunny moved forward, grinning. His wet lips shone in the sunlight. As hard as she could, Mina shoved Kegs backward. He staggered against his bag-of-bones friend and they fell against the back door swearing.

Mina snatched up the watch and ran.

Pieces of a Lie was longlisted for the Ned Kelly Award for Crime Fiction 2015.

First published October 2014 ©

About the Book

To find her father she must choose...destroy herself or the only man who believes in her. The closer Mina gets to the truth the more she acts like a suspect and when someone dies Detective Lincoln Drummond must confront his worst fear — that the woman he loves is a cold-hearted killer.

Find out more on my website

Available on

Amazon

iBooks

Kobo

Print copies available through my website and from select retailers. See all buy links

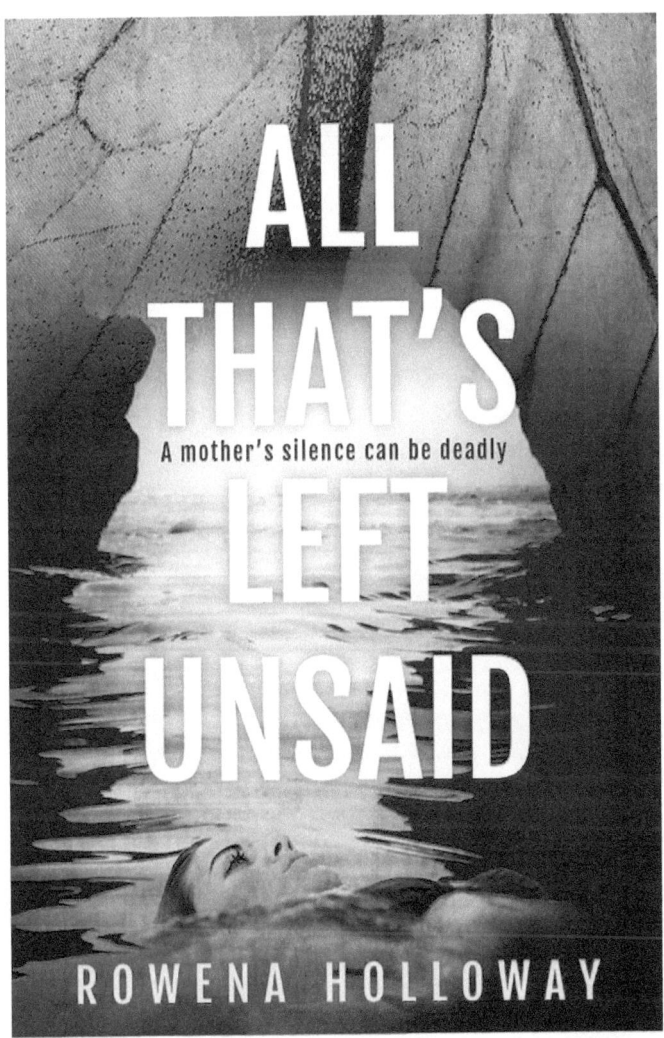

ALL THAT'S

A mother's silence can be deadly

LEFT

UNSAID

ROWENA HOLLOWAY

all that's left
unsaid

First Chapter Extract

Before

THERE ARE PERIODS WHEN HE manages to
forget. A few hours at first. Soon a whole day, a
week. Finally, a month of sleep-filled nights. Then
it returns in a great wave of memory. All it takes is
a word, a scent, the chill of wind on wet skin.

It begins with the slap of water against granite
and the mineral-tinged odour of dank stone. He
recalls the glistening drops of water, and lingers
on the image of her exposed flesh. Then he's
jerked awake by her echoing scream.

From the beach it hadn't seemed so far, and
in the Mediterranean heat the blue waters off
Positano were inviting.

'It'll be an adventure,' he'd told her.

'You just want an excuse to get me into that

skimpy bikini.' She had smiled up at him with the adoration of early love and no inkling of what was to come.

He'd been the first to reach deep water. Always one to test himself, he dived, intent on reaching the weedy bottom. The ocean tugged at his hair. He dove down until he felt ready to burst beneath the weight of water. Self-preservation made him kick for the surface. Through a veil of saturated hair, he gasped for air.

She was still swimming out to meet him. Hers was the sedate, hesitant stroke of someone unfamiliar with the ocean; but she wouldn't make a fuss—she never did. It was why he'd chosen her. Her faith in him was boundless.

He gazed at the postcard-perfect sky, and waited. The monolithic cliff towered skyward. Wind fluted through the breaks and crevices in its craggy face. Birds swooped and soared, then hung in the air currents that swept the scraggy brink. Their caws and squawks were like a warning.

By the time she reached him, she gasped and sputtered as water stirred by wind and tide smacked at her lips.

'It's so cold.'

'I know a way we can warm up.' He winked as

they trod water in the choppy swell. 'Didn't that old woman say the cave was once a place for lover's trysts?'

That made her snort and she pushed his head beneath the water. In retaliation, he grabbed her ankles and pulled her down for a salty kiss. When they surfaced, breathless and spluttering, she reminded him of the other myth about the cave.

'Find me the gold and I might let you cop a feel.' Then she laughed: they'd already done much more than that.

They swam on, battling the sea's efforts to hold them back, their exertions doing little to ward off the chill. By the time they reached the shallow arch of the cave entrance, the tide was high and the opening almost submerged.

'Are you sure this is a good idea?' Her jaw trembled as she spoke. It could have been the cold, though he felt it, too—that uneasy sense that something wasn't quite right; but there was no way he'd turn back now.

'Come on. We've come this far.'

Inside, it was dank and close. Seawater smacked against the jagged edge of a granite shelf. Suffuse light filtered through a fissure in the stony ceiling, and cast shadows on walls so flinty that in places they seemed serrated. As he hauled himself out, he tasted that unforgettable, mineral-tinged dankness.

He helped her onto the rocky shelf. Her white bathing suit hid nothing, and glistening droplets slid off her rosy, goose-fleshed body. She trembled when he touched her, but as he reached for her sodden bathing suit, she stopped him.

'It feels like someone's watching,' she whispered.

He made a show of searching the cave. In the far reaches, beneath the ceiling fissure and the narrow beam of sunlight, he found a chasm as deep as a well. She stood not far away, shivering, her arms wrapped around herself, eyes huge as she gazed at the solid walls of the cavern.

'This seems like an ideal place to stash some gold.'

He'd meant it as a joke, but as his eyes adjusted to the light he saw something glimmer. A group of small stones lay scattered nearby. He snatched one up, tossed it in, and counted the seconds until it hit the bottom with a sharp crack. He calculated the depth was about twice his height, just shy of four metres.

She only agreed to climb down because he was

strong enough to haul her up again. That she might slip and fall never occurred to him. Neither of them considered what they would do if he couldn't reach her. Fed by the local myths, excitement made them reckless.

Halfway down, she called, 'I think it's a bracelet. I'll try and—'

A tumble of stones—her panicked shriek.

In the smear of sunlight he could just make her out, curled on her side, motionless. Frantic, he called her name. When she finally moved, using words he thought would never pass her lips, he laughed with relief.

'I like this foul-mouthed side of you,' he told her.

'Shut up. There's something else down here.'

Then her scream split the cave.

Nominated for Readers Choice Award AusRomToday.com 2015

First published April 2015 ©

About the Book

All my life I've waited for my mother's affection. Now I must compete with a dead woman.

Intrigued to learn her mother once lived in Italy, a secret she has kept for thirty years, Harriet (Harrie) Taylor accepts the challenge to determine if the remains known only as the Positano Skeleton belong to her mother's long-lost friend. It's as good an excuse as any to escape Australia and the stench of career failure. Yet Harrie finds beautiful Positano isn't quite the sun-soaked paradise of the holiday brochures and when a homeless man hands her a photograph, Harrie is forced to question how far she will go to find the truth.

Find out more on my website

Available on

Amazon

iBooks

Kobo

Print copies available through my website and from select retailers. See all buy links

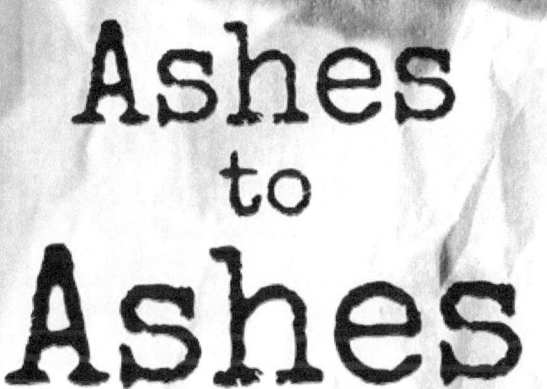

Ashes
to
Ashes

Death is just the beginning...

ROWENA
HOLLOWAY

ashes to ashes

First Chapter Extract

Allie

Fear should have kept me safe.

I knew better than to open the door without checking the peephole. In the frenzy of dinner preparations and the excitement of sharing Christmas with the two people I loved most, I'd forgotten to be cautious. When the door knocker echoed down the hallway I'd been so wrapped up in baking cakes, decorating trees and expecting guests that I'd done little more than worry they were early.

Only it wasn't them.

At first I thought it was a motorcycle courier with a late delivery. I smiled, polite even to evil. It was only when he shoved me back and stepped inside that I realised what he had in mind had nothing to do with Christmas.

Did I try to run? I hope so. I hope I fought and screamed and left at least some trace of DNA on that bastard's clothing. But I couldn't have. Babs from next door would have been banging on the wall at the slightest sound, and I knew she was home because Bing Crosby had been crooning about a White Christmas all damn day.

All I really remember is the darkness as he slipped the mask over my face and the tightness of the rope which wasn't a rope but something thinner and slicker and I realised he'd used my own Christmas lights to tie me up. Christmas lights! Even in the throes of terror, while he screamed in my face from behind that motorcycle helmet, I thought of how everyone would laugh when they found me—if they found me—while he kept ranting at me about something I couldn't understand. Just as I couldn't understand what was happening. Or why it was happening. And why to me?

Then he vanished. A door slammed. Knowing he was gone made it easier to focus and I struggled to free myself, but the more I fought against them the tighter the bounds became. It got harder and harder to breathe. He'd slipped the cord around my throat so that every twist of my hands tightened the noose. No matter how hard I tried the flex wouldn't loosen. My own stupid fault. Egotistical idiot! I couldn't have bought a cheap set of lights like every other year. Oh, no. I had to impress.

Footsteps thudded overhead. He hadn't left. And if he was still here, he could come back. I struggled harder against my ties. Free. I had to get free. Get help.

And then the glass shattered. He'd thrown my Orrefors crystal vase against the wall. It sat on the little half table at the top of the stairs and was my only memento of my barely remembered mother. And he'd smashed it. Swearing tumbled down the stairs as he stomped toward my bedroom. Another crash. He was going through my things.

I knew then who had sent him. And why.

God help me, for a moment I wished it was Charlotte here tied to the chair. My nose and throat filled with mucus from useless tears. I called myself a stupid lazy bitch, to stop crying and get myself free.

My heart pounded and sweat dripped into my eyes because the hood was so tight and the central heating had been going all day joined by the heat from the oven because I'd only just opened the door to put the roast in when I heard the knocking. As I struggled I thought of all the food still waiting to go in, that there was no way it would be ready in time. You see, I was in denial even then.

I was soon drenched with sweat but that only made it harder to get free. From upstairs came a high-pitched bellow of rage. More crashes, this time from the room above me that I used as an office. He'd never find what he was after. Charlotte had it all. Everything except the evidence on my phone. Without that her proof would be thin, but I'd wanted to show it to her when we met, to give Charlotte a big surprise.

Charlotte. I always put her first.

In all of my thirty years I never properly considered my own needs, always deferred to what others wanted, always suffered from being so perpetually nice that everyone took me for granted. Even those who loved me, like Charlotte.

Why did I only understand that when gripped by terror?

I prayed then for someone to come, that Charlotte or Drew would rescue me.

But what if they come and he's still here? I thought. And then I thought, *What if they didn't?*

Bing finally stopped crooning so I screamed as loud as I could and stomped my feet, mercifully free of cord. I screamed and stomped though the mask probably stifled my cries just as the rug muted my thuds. With all my strength I tried to jump the chair toward the adjoining wall so I could kick against the spot where I knew Babs would be lying on her couch, sipping whiskey and waiting for Bing to resume his serenade.

It was no good. Wingback chairs weren't designed that way.

The distinctive ringtone I'd assigned Charlotte burst from the kitchen. I had a moment of hope then it splintered, like the vase. The call meant she wasn't coming. She'd never send a text to let me down.

The racket upstairs stopped.

Why hadn't I chosen a soft classical piece for her ringtone instead of that frenetic dance music? The beast upstairs was bound to hear it. He'd find the phone and the videos I took and all my efforts, all the fear I'd faced down to help Charlotte get what she wanted, would be for nothing. Oh why hadn't I uploaded those videos to the Cloud? After last night's fright I'd meant to, but I'd been trembling so much after running from the station, my steps echoed by others, that I'd been too terrified to reveal my presence with even the dull glow of a computer screen. And later, when I finally had the courage to peek through my curtains and saw the street deserted, I'd laughed at myself for freaking out at the ghostly echo of my own footsteps.

But they hadn't been an echo, had they? I'd been right to be afraid. And if I hadn't laughed myself out it, if I hadn't been so preoccupied with making the perfect meal, I might have looked through my damn peephole before I flung open my front door.

The ringing stopped. In the hollow silence I wished she'd ring again. Would it really be so bad if he found the phone? He hadn't taken off his helmet. If I couldn't identify him and he had what he wanted he'd leave me alone. I clung to that hope as I strained against my bonds. The cord must have stretched a little because it slipped. Not much. Just enough to keep my hope alive.

I'd barely loosened my arms when his footsteps pounded the stairs.

Then he was there in front of me, yelling again, his anger muffled by that dark helmet. No longer caring that he could see me I strained harder against the bonds, desperate to be free, furious at being so bloody pathetic and determined that my last sight of anyone would not be this angry bastard!

My head pounded so ferociously I could hardly string two thoughts together, and with every twist of my hands the cord around my neck tightened until all I could hear was the throbbing of my arteries. It was so hard to breathe. The pounding got worse. Everything began to blur.

A white light filled my vision, getting brighter and brighter, and the hammer stopped knocking against the inside of my skull, and my head felt like it was filled with helium until I was floating in a void. No colour. No sound. No sense of anything. Fleetingly I thought of Charlotte, left alone and grieving, eaten up with guilt. The light in my head broke apart, became a million little candle flames, and I saw balloons...

Balloons at a birthday party...

Daddy telling her to blow out the candles...

And Mother was happy. Sober. And even though I was little again, and joyous at all the presents, with no clue about my future, I was thinking, *This can't be the end, not when my life is just beginning.*

Coming in April 2016

Join my Suspense Community to stay in the loop
and be the first to get all the news, reviews, and
interviews from rowenaholloway.com

acknowledgements

Writing may be a solitary activity, yet the journey is buoyed by the wings of others.

If not for the support and encouragement—and the homework—from my writing groups I doubt some of these stories would ever have been written. My thanks go to The Henley Scribblers and Seaside Writers for the inspiration and feedback (and Tim Tams) that helped me find my feet. Love and appreciation to Diane Hester, Alison Manthorpe, Mary Gudzenovs, Helen Van Rooijen and Kathy Blacker, the Eyre Writers novelists, who took a chance on this ring-in, held my hand in the early days and have been there ever since. I'm especially indebted to my regular girl-possie, Claire Laishley and Pamela Mosel, for all the laughter, insights and gentle shoves that got me here. And a huge thank you to Sandy Vaile, my Suspense Sister, for sharing the journey.

To all those authors whose beautiful words keep me inspired and longing to improve, please keep writing.

And to my readers, thank you for welcoming my strange tales into your homes.

about the author

Rowena Holloway is an Australian writer of novels and short stories. Before settling on writing as a career, Rowena apprenticed as a hairdresser, played at receptionist in an engineering firm, indulged her love of learning by obtaining a handful of degrees, including a PhD in business, and was a tenured university lecturer. All of which convinced her fiction writing was preferable to the real world. Under the working title of Out of the Abyss, her first novel was a semi-finalist in the 2010 Amazon Breakthrough Novel Award. Her short stories have been included in the Stringybark anthology Yellow Pearl and the 2011 Anthology of Award Winning Australian Writing.

Rowena also tracks down leading authors and interviews them, and reviews fiction across a range of genres. All of which can be found on her website http://www.rowenaholloway.com

Connect on Facebook: https://www.facebook.com/ rowenahollowayauthor

Connect on twitter: https://twitter.com/ RowenaHolloway

If you've enjoyed this book, share the love and show your appreciation by writing a review on Goodreads, Amazon or iBooks.

praise for
rowena
holloway

Praise for All That's Left Unsaid

"*...plenty of surprises and a very clever twist at the end... the final scene brought me to tears.*" Sandy Vaile, suspense author

"*...a spectacular story in every sense of the word – as dramatic and as breathtaking as the setting of Positano, on Italy's Amalfi Coast.*" Jenn J McLeod, author

"*This was a great mystery that kept you guessing to the very end! I was never able to figure out who was lying and who was telling the truth. Everything all came together nicely in the end.*" Amy on Goodreads

"*Loads of twists and turns. Love the flavours of Italy.*" Susan G on Goodreads

"*This was a fabulous, on the edge of your seat read. Loads of gorgeous, beautifully written detail and a fabulous cast of well written characters.*" Tamara M on Goodreads

Praise for Pieces of a Lie

"...*combines* noir *with romantic suspense and does it solidly*" WriteNoteReviews

"...*enough twists and turns to keep the reader in suspense*" Meredith Jaffe, Books Reviewer, The Hoopla.

"*Rowena Holloway is a master of hook chapter endings...plenty of surprises and a very clever twist at the end.*" Sandy Vaile, suspense author.

"*This debut come with a very macabre twist ... one that is best not read while one is alone in semi-darkness.*" Kathryn White, author.

"*It drew me in the from the very first page. Rowena Holloway is a talented author. Recommended.*" Geraldine Evans UK crime writer.

"*A breathless slalom of hair-pin turns and never-saw-'em-coming surprises. Worth every minute of sleep I lost staying up to all hours reading it!*" Diane Hester, Suspense Author.